THE
GOLDEN CAGE

For Mal – I.J.
For Sally Maidment – K.B.

Text copyright © 1994 by Ivan Jones. Illustrations copyright © 1994 by Ken Brown

The rights of Ivan Jones and Ken Brown to be identified as the author and illustrator of this work have
been asserted by them in accordance with the Copyright, Designs and Patents Act, 1988.
First published in Great Britain in 1994 by Andersen Press Ltd.,
20 Vauxhall Bridge Road, London SW1V 2SA.
This paperback edition first published in 1999 by Andersen Press Ltd.
Published in Australia by Random House Australia Pty., 20 Alfred Street, Milsons Point,
Sydney, NSW 2061. All rights reserved. Colour separated in Switzerland by Photolitho AG,
Gossau, Zürich. Printed and bound in Italy by Grafiche AZ, Verona.

10   9   8   7   6   5   4   3   2   1

British Library Cataloguing in Publication Data available.

ISBN 0 86264 844 0
This book has been printed on acid-free paper

THE GOLDEN CAGE

By Ivan Jones

Illustrated by Ken Brown

Andersen Press · London

In a big, beautiful old house in the middle of a park, there lived a little girl called Abigail. Abigail had a rich mother and father and everything she asked for.

But Abigail was lonely. She spent hours watching people come and go up the gravel drive. There were plenty of visitors for her mum and dad. But none for her.

One afternoon, when she was walking in the gardens, Abigail heard
a bird singing in an oak tree.

"What's that bird?" she called to the old gardener.

"That's the songthrush," said the gardener. "The best singer in the garden."

"Oh, I wish I had a bird like that who would sing to me all the time!" cried Abigail. "Then I wouldn't be so alone. You must catch him for me!"

"Catch him, Miss?" asked the gardener. "But why?"

"So that I can keep him with me in a cage, of course."

"That's cruel, keeping a wild bird in a cage," he chided.

"How *dare* you say such a thing!" Abigail shouted, stamping her foot. "I *shall* have him!"

The old gardener sighed. He knew he must do as he was told.

So that night he laid a trap and caught the songthrush.

The next morning, Abigail burst into the gardener's shed. She clapped her hands in triumph when she saw the little wooden cage in the corner.

"You're my best friend!" she shrieked at the songthrush. "Every day I'll talk to you, and you will sing for me."

Then she rudely grabbed the cage and ran off.

"Sing to me! Sing!" she yelled at the bird in the cage. The songthrush twisted and turned, this way and that. But he didn't sing.

At the end of the day, Abigail snapped her fingers. "I know why you won't sing for me!" she cried. "You don't like this dirty little wooden cage."

So she sent for one that was bigger and better.

"There!" she cried. "A *silver* cage. Now you'll sing!"

All that day, the songthrush poked his head through the bars of the silver cage and flapped his wings. But still he didn't sing.

"I know why you won't sing!" said Abigail that evening. "You don't like this cramped silver cage."

So she sent for one that was bigger and better.

"There!" she cried. "A *golden* cage for your golden voice. Now I *know* you'll sing!"

The songthrush huddled in a corner of the cage. His eyes grew dull, his feathers drooped. And still he didn't sing.

"You stupid bird!" shouted Abigail. "I've given you everything you could ever want." She snatched up the golden cage and banged it down in front of the gardener.

"What's the matter with him?" she demanded. "Why won't he sing?"

The gardener peered into the cage. "He's very unhappy. He's going to die," said the old man sadly.

"Die?" shouted Abigail. "He can't die. He's mine!"

"But he will die, unless you let him go."

"No!" shrieked Abigail and seizing the golden cage, she ran off into the wood.

Abigail ran and ran. The cage grew heavy.

At last she threw herself down to rest in a mossy clearing. It was very quiet. She looked around her. On every tree, on every bush, she saw birds; hundreds of birds, all watching her. She felt frightened. She looked down at the golden cage.

"I only wanted him to sing for me," she said.

"For me, for me," came an echo of her voice.

Suddenly all the birds flocked into the air. They swooped down and thronged about her in a mass of wings and beaks and claws. They closed in. It went dark. Abigail shouted in fear. She tried to push her way out of the cage of birds, but they held her fast.

"Let me out!" she cried.

"Let me out!" came the echo. "Let me out! Let me out!"

Abigail flung herself to the ground. She kicked and yelled and threatened and howled. But the birds still held her prisoner. She stood up and pleaded with them to let her free.

But the birds still held her prisoner.

Abigail sank down, exhausted. She cried for her mother and father. Through her tears she saw the golden cage beside her, gleaming strangely. She felt through the bars with her fingers. The songthrush lay very still and quiet.

"What have I done?" she sobbed, as she opened the golden door. She reached into the cage for the songthrush and held him on her outstretched palm.

"Fly away, little golden voice," she said.

As soon as the songthrush flew from her hand, the woodland birds scattered, whirling and wheeling in fantastic patterns. Abigail watched silently. Then she began the long walk home.

The next day, Abigail sat alone in the garden. The old gardener came and squatted beside her.

"I'm sorry," she said.

He nodded and smiled. Then, overhead in the big oak tree, they heard a little bird with a golden voice singing!

"It's the songthrush!" cried Abigail.

"Perhaps because you set him free you've found a friend, after all," said the gardener.

And from that time on, the songthrush came to Abigail's garden
every day and sang her its beautiful golden song.

More Andersen Press paperback picture books!

OUR PUPPY'S HOLIDAY
by Ruth Brown

SCRATCH 'N' SNIFF
by Gus Clarke

NOTHING BUT TROUBLE
by Gus Clarke

FRIGHTENED FRED
by Peta Coplans

THE HILL AND THE ROCK
by David McKee

MR UNDERBED
by Chris Riddell

WHAT DO YOU WANT TO BE, BRIAN?
by Jeanne Willis and Mary Rees

MICHAEL
by Tony Bradman and Tony Ross

THE LONG BLUE BLAZER
by Jeanne Willis and Susan Varley

FROG IS A HERO
by Max Velthuijs